This
Treasure Cove Story
belongs to

SLEEPING BEAUTY
AND THE GOOD FAIRIES

A CENTUM BOOK 978-1-912396-17-7
Published in Great Britain by Centum Books Ltd.
This edition published 2019.

1 3 5 7 9 10 8 6 4 2

Centum Books Ltd, 20 Devon Square, Newton Abbot,
Devon, TQ12 2HR, UK.

www.centumbooksltd.co.uk | books@centumbooksltd.co.uk
CENTUM BOOKS Limited Reg. No. 07641486.

A CIP catalogue record for this book is available
from the British Library.

Printed in China.

A Treasure Cove Story

WALT DISNEY'S
Sleeping Beauty
AND THE GOOD FAIRIES

By Dorothy Strebe and Annie North Bedford
Pictures Van the Walt Disney Studio
Adapted by Julius Svendsen and C W Satterfield

A happy bustle filled the cottage in the woods. The three good fairies, Flora, Fauna and Merryweather, were flying about the place, as busy as merry, buzzing bees. For the first time since her marriage to Prince Phillip, Princess Aurora was coming to visit them!

So Flora waved her wand over the woodland
flowers until each blossom glowed like a bit of rainbow.
Fauna worked her magic on the baby birds,
teaching them to twitter a welcome song.

And Merryweather, with the help of the breezes,
swept and dusted the little cottage until it shone
with a magic glow.

It was in this very cottage that the three fairies had raised the little princess from her christening day. And now she was coming to visit them here. And they were to go on with her to the castle of the King and Queen, to deck it out with magic for the homecoming feast.

It was Merryweather who first heard the *clippety-clop* of distant hooves and the rumble of wheels on the royal coach, far down the forest road.

'Come, come, girls!' Merryweather cried. 'She's almost here. There's no time to lose!'

Quickly she bent over the well beside the
cottage for a glance at her reflection in the water
below. *Plink!* Into the well fell her magic wand.
But Merryweather was too excited to notice that.

Up bustled Fauna, puffing just a bit. 'Oh my!' she cried. 'Do I look all right?'

Over the well she bent for a glimpse. But just then, the coachman's horn sounded loud and clear, off amongst the trees. So Fauna did not hear the *plink* as her magic wand dropped into the well.

Next came Flora, trying to be calm.

'The dear girl,' she fluttered. 'How sweet of her to want to see us and the cottage again. But remember, we must not keep her long. For the King and Queen will be waiting at the castle.'

As she spoke, she caught sight of the royal
carriage approaching at last.

'Oh,' she cried. 'Is my cap on straight?'

She bent to look, then turned towards the road
as the coach came to a halt. And into the well,
all unseen, fell a third magic wand!

'Flora! Fauna! Merryweather!' cried a voice
they loved. And down from the coach stepped
Princess Aurora, into the good fairies' arms.

Together they went into the little cottage where
they had lived for so many happy years.

'How lovely it is,' said the happy princess. 'Just
as I remembered it – and so are you sweet three!'

'Well, my dear,' said Flora briskly. 'Now we must
all be on our way. For your father and mother have
kindly invited us to come to the castle with you,
and to decorate it for the homecoming feast.'

'Lovely,' said the princess. 'You'll decorate it with your magic wands. Where are they, by the way?'

'Right here,' said Merryweather. 'Why, we wouldn't be without them, you know.'

'No indeed,' said Fauna. 'Always right at hand…'

'But they aren't!' said Flora. 'Where are those wands?'

Well, they looked high and low, inside the cottage and out. But not a sign of them could they find.

'We cannot disappoint the King and Queen,'
cried Merryweather.

'And everyone in the countryside,' added Fauna.

'We must find them!' said Flora firmly. 'Now
let's think. What were we doing last with them?'

'You were brightening up the woodland flowers,' said Merryweather.

So they hunted through the woods. But Flora's wand was not there.

'You were teaching the baby birds a welcome song,' they reminded Fauna.

So they hunted among the bushes and trees. They searched every bird's nest around. But Fauna's wand was not there.

'You, Merryweather, were sweeping out the cottage with the help of the little breezes.'

So they hunted all through the cottage again. But the wand was nowhere to be seen.

Now the sun was sinking beyond the deep woods.
At the castle, everyone would be waiting, they knew.
What in the world could they do?

'I know,' said Princess Aurora. 'I'll ask the
Wishing Well.'

So over the Wishing Well's edge she bent.

'Why, it's all a-sparkle with sunbeams,' she
cried. 'And starlight and rainbows – deep inside
the well!'

'Our wands!' cried the fairies.

Tugging together on the rope, they pulled
up the bucket in the well. Up it came, full to the
brim with magic wands and sunbeams and such.

Then into the carriage the four of them flew. And away went the horses, *clippety-clop*, off to the castle. It soon was aglow with sunbeams and starlight… and lovelight, too, for Princess Aurora's homecoming. And a lovely time was had by all.

Treasure Cove Stories

1 Three Little Pigs
2 Snow White and
the Seven Dwarfs
3 The Fox and the Hound
- Hide-and-Seek
4 Dumbo
5 Cinderella
6 Cinderella's Friends
7 Alice in Wonderland
8 Mad Hatter's Tea Party
from Alice in Wonderland
9 Mickey Mouse and
his Spaceship
10 Peter Pan
11 Pinocchio
12 Mickey and the Beanstalk
13 Sleeping Beauty
and the Good Fairies
14 The Lucky Puppy
15 Chicken Little
16 The Incredibles
17 Coco
18 Winnie-the-Pooh and Tigger
19 The Sword in the Stone
20 Mary Poppins
21 The Jungle Book
22 The Aristocats
23 Lady and the Tramp
24 Bambi
25 Bambi - Friends of the Forest
26 Pete's Dragon
27 Beauty and the Beast
- The Teapot's Tale
28 Monsters, Inc.
- M is for Monster
29 Finding Nemo
30 Incredibles 2
31 The Incredibles
- Jack-Jack Attack
32 Mother Goose
33 Wall·E
34 Up
35 The Princess and the Frog
36 Toy Story
- The Pet Problem
37 I am Dumbo
38 Dora the Explorer
- Grandma's House

39 Spider-Man
- Night of the Vulture!
40 Wreck-it Ralph
41 Wreck-it Ralph 2
- Ralph Breaks the Internet
42 The Invincible Iron Man
- Eye of the Dragon
43 SpongeBob SquarePants
- Sponge in Space!
44 Blaze and the Monster Machines
- Let's be Firefighters!
45 Toy Story
- A Roaring Adventure
46 Cars - Deputy Mater Saves the Day!
47 The Amazing Spider-Man
- Trapped by the Green Goblin!
48 Big Hero 6
49 Spider-Man - High Voltage!
50 Frozen
51 Cinderella is my Babysitter
52 Beauty and the Beast
- I am the Beast
53 Blaze and the Monster Machines
- Mighty Monster Machines
54 Blaze and the Monster Machines
- Dino Parade!
55 Teenage Mutant Ninja Turtles
- Follow the Ninja!
56 I am a Princess
57 The Big Book of Paw Patrol
58 Paw Patrol
- Adventures with Grandpa!
59 Paw Patrol - Pirate Pups!
60 Trolls
61 Trolls Holiday
62 The Secret Life of Pets
63 Zootropolis
64 Ariel is my Babysitter
65 Tiana is my Babysitter
66 Belle is my Babysitter
67 Paw Patrol - Itty-Bitty Kitty Rescue
68 Moana
69 Nella the Princess Knight
- My Heart is Bright!
70 Guardians of the Galaxy
71 Captain America
- High-Stakes Heist!
72 Ant-Man

73 The Mighty Avengers
74 The Mighty Avengers
- Lights Out!
75 The Incredible Hulk
76 Shimmer & Shine
- Wish Upon a Sleepover
77 Shimmer & Shine
- Backyard Ballet
78 Paw Patrol - All-Star Pups!
79 Teenage Mutant Ninja Turtles
- Really Spaced Out!
80 I am Ariel
81 Madagascar
82 Jasmine is my Babysitter
83 How to Train your Dragon
84 Shrek
85 Puss in Boots
86 Kung Fu Panda
87 Beauty and the Beast
- I am Belle
88 The Lion Guard
- The Imaginary Okapi
89 Thor - Thunder Strike!
90 Guardians of the Galaxy
- Rocket to the Rescue!
91 Nella the Princess Knight
- Nella and the Dragon
92 Shimmer & Shine
- Treasure Twins!
93 Olaf's Frozen Adventure
94 Black Panther
95 Trolls
-Branch's Bunker Birthday
96 Trolls - Poppy's Party
97 The Ugly Duckling
98 Cars - Look Out for Mater!
99 101 Dalmatians
100 The Sorcerer's Apprentice
101 Tangled
102 Avengers
- The Threat of Thanos
103 Puppy Dog Pals
- Don't Rain on my Pug-Rade
104 Jurassic Park
105 The Mighty Thor
106 Doctor Strange
107 Captain Marvel

Book list may be subject to change.